# Half as Big

## Lily Hyde
### Illustrated by Karen Perrins

A & C Black • London

White Wolves series consultant: Sue Ellis,
Centre for Literacy in Primary Education

This book can be used in the White Wolves Guided Reading
programme by readers of average ability in Year 2

Text copyright © 2010 Lily Hyde
Illustrations copyright © 2010 Karen Perrins

The rights of Lily Hyde and Karen Perrins to be identified
as the author and illustrator of this work has been asserted by them
in accordance with the Copyrights, Designs and Patents Act 1988.

ISBN 978-1-4081-2842-8

A CIP catalogue for this book is available from the British Library.

This book is produced using paper that is made from wood
grown in managed, sustainable forests. It is natural, renewable
and recyclable. The logging and manufacturing processes conform
to the environmental regulations of the country of origin.

Printed and bound in China by C&C Offset Printing Co.

# Chapter One

"I'm tired of being a big fish in a small pond," Medio Pollito said one day. "I'm off to the city to see the king."

"I'm not sure that's wise, dear," said his mother.

Her son wasn't a big fish in a small pond. In their large chicken yard, he was the smallest chicken.

In fact, Medio Pollito was only *half* a chick. He had just one leg, one wing and one eye. But to make up for being so small, he thought twice as much of himself.

"Of course it's wise," he said. "I'm so important, the king will be glad to see me!"

"All right, dear," said his mother. "Just two words of advice: be polite and helpful to everyone you meet, and keep away from the cook in the king's kitchen."

Medio Pollito took no notice. He was much too important to listen to his mother.

# Chapter Two

Beside the road to the city was a stream. It was full of rubbish thrown in by people walking past.

"Help!" the stream water cried to Medio Pollito. "I'm so choked up with rubbish, I can't move. Please clear some of it away for me, kind half-chick."

"I'm too important to do that," said Medio Pollito. "Clear up your own mess!"

On he went, until he came to a smoky bonfire by the road.

"Help!" the fire called. "I'm about to go out. Please put some more wood on me, nice half-chick."

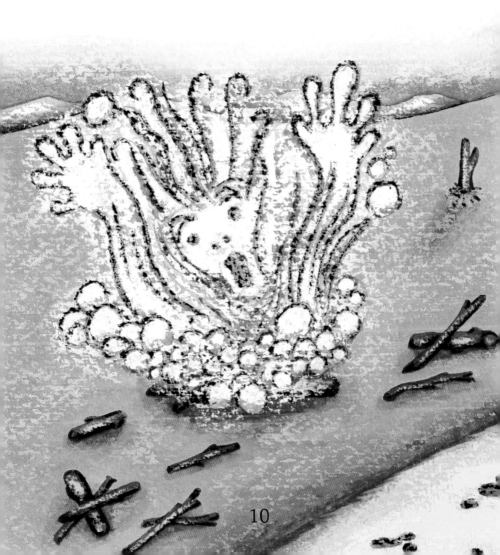

"I'm going to see the king. I can't stop for you," said Medio Pollito. "Get your own wood!"

A little further along was a tree with
a breeze caught in its branches.

"Help!" the breeze shouted. "I lost
my way and now I'm stuck in this tree.
Please release me, dear half-chick."

"I haven't any time to waste, the king is waiting for me!" said Medio Pollito. "Find your own way out." And on he hopped to the city.

# Chapter Three

The city was a lot bigger than the chicken yard Medio Pollito had left behind. Thousands of people rushed this way and that.

The only place they stopped was in front of the cathedral, where they bowed politely to the saints before hurrying on.

"Hello, are you lost?" the saints asked,
when they saw Medio Pollito.

"Of course not! I'm going to see the
king," replied Medio Pollito. "Not that it's
any of *your* business."

"You should go home, dear, the city is no place for a half-chick like you."

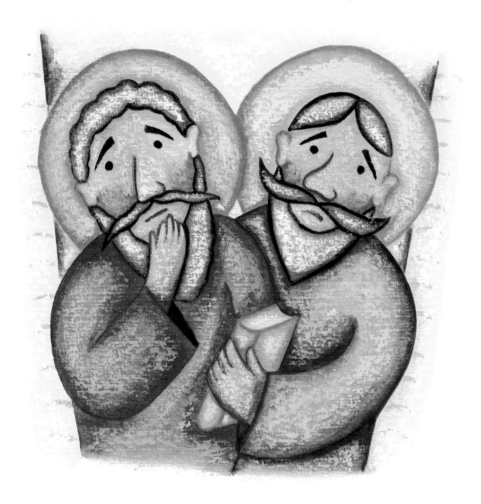

Medio Pollito took no notice. He was much too important to listen to some old saints.

When at last he came to the king's palace, he looked through an open window. There, he caught sight of the cook wearing a great, high snow-white hat.

18

That must be the king! thought Medio
Pollito. He flapped his one wing and
blinked his one eye, crowing as loudly as
he could: "Look at me!"

The king's cook looked out of the window. "You're just what I need," he said, "for the king's dinner."

Then he grabbed Medio Pollito and threw him in the cooking pot.

# Chapter Four

The water in the pot was so hot, it scalded Medio Pollito's feathers. "Help!" he cried. "Please, water, stop boiling me."

"Why should I help you?" said the water. "You didn't help me when I was choked up with rubbish. Get yourself out of this mess."

Medio Pollito made an enormous jump, and managed to jump out of the cooking pot ... and into the fire, which began to burn his feathers.

"Help!" he shouted. "Please, fire, stop scorching me."

"Why should I?" said the fire. "You didn't help me when I was going out. Get yourself out of this pickle."

Just then, the king's cook saw what was happening. "What a scrawny half-chick!" he said. "Now I see you're not good enough to serve up to the king."

He picked Medio Pollito out of the flames and tossed him through the window. "You might as well go back where I found you."

# Chapter Five

A breeze caught hold of Medio Pollito. At first it was lovely and cool on his burnt feathers, but then it bowled him along and blasted him up to the rooftops.

"Help!" he cried. "Please stop blowing me around like a bit of rubbish, breeze, and take me home to my chicken yard."

"Why should I?" said the breeze. "You wouldn't help me when I was caught in a tree. Find your own way home."

It blew Medio Pollito up to the top of the cathedral tower – and left him there.

"Hello, dear," said the saints. "Didn't we say the city was no place for you? But you thought too much of yourself to listen. Now you'll have to stay up here for ever."

Medio Pollito found he couldn't move his leg from the top of the tower. The breeze spun him round and round. Medio Pollito had become a weather vane!

"Serves you right," said the saints.

The wind was cold up on the tower.
The rain soaked Medio Pollito and the
sun roasted him. Down below, all the busy
people stopped to bow politely to the saints
on the front of the cathedral. Then they
stopped a little longer, and looked a little
higher at the weather vane, to see which
way the wind was blowing.

Medio Pollito flapped his one wing and blinked his one eye. He crowed as loudly as he could: "Look at me! I'm so important that *everyone* is glad to see me!"